To remember what you've read, write your initials in a square!

DATE DUE		3/15
APR 29 2015		
5/15/18		

USE YOUR WORDS, SOPHIE!

ROSEMARY WELLS

VIKING
An Imprint of Penguin Group (USA)

For Squell, Spo, Rocious, Tick-tock, and Feeb

VIKING
Published by the Penguin Group
Penguin Group (USA) LLC
375 Hudson Street
New York, New York 10014

USA / Canada / UK / Ireland / Australia
New Zealand / India / South Africa / China

penguin.com
A Penguin Random House Company

First published in the United States of America by Viking,
an imprint of Penguin Young Readers Group, 2015

LIBRARY OF CONGRESS CATALOGING-IN-PUBLICATION DATA
Wells, Rosemary, author, illustrator.
Use your words, Sophie! / by Rosemary Wells.
pages cm
Summary: "When Sophie's new sister won't stop crying, only two-year-old Sophie can communicate
with her, even if she isn't using her words as her parents want her to"—Provided by publisher.
ISBN 978-0-670-01663-1 (hardcover)
[1. Babies—Fiction. 2. Sisters—Fiction. 3. Communication—Fiction. 4. Names, Personal—Fiction.]
I. Title.
PZ7.W46843Us 2015
[E]—dc23
2014011450

Manufactured in China

1   3   5   7   9   10   8   6   4   2

Set in LTC Kennerley Pro
The art for this book was created using ink, watercolor, and gouache on watercolor paper.

Sophie's mama brought a small bundle back from the hospital.
In it was a brand-new pink-nosed baby.
"Her name will be Ashleigh," said Sophie's mama.

Sophie's daddy clattered in the front door with the changing
table, the bassinet, the stroller, and the bathtub.
"Sophie!" he said.
"Say hello to your new sister, Amber."

"We decided on Ashleigh," said Mama.
"Amber," said Daddy.
 Sophie said hello to her new sister in Jellyfish language.
"Use your words, please, Sophie," said Mama.

It was time for Ashleigh Amber's lunch.
Sophie told her sister how to use the big girl cup.
"Use your words, please, Sophie!" said Sophie's daddy.

Ashleigh Amber was swaddled up
for her nap in her bassinet. She smiled sweetly.
"Nap time for Sophie, too!" said Sophie's mama.

But this was day one of Sophie's being too old for naps.
"No! No! No!" growled Sophie in Hyena language.
"Use your words, please, Sophie," said Sophie's daddy.

Sophie's daddy tucked Sophie into her big girl bed.
He put her sparkly iguana on the pillow next to Sophie.
"Rest time, darling girl," said Sophie's daddy.

Sophie sang the Baboon national anthem
in her bed as loud as she could possibly sing.

In the next room, Ashleigh Amber woke up.

She yelled so loud that
Sophie had to put on her space helmet.
Daddy had to call Granny.

Granny said she'd come over.

Sophie said hello to Granny in Space language.
"Use your words, please, darling girl," said Sophie's mama.
Granny said, "Hello, Sophie," in Martian.

"Now what's this baby's name?" Granny asked.
"It's going to be Samantha Marie," said Sophie's mama.

Daddy did not like the name Samantha Marie.
He consulted his name book.
"Meet Symphonie Pearl!" said Sophie's daddy.

"First," said Granny, "let's see if we can quiet her down."
Mama tried feeding Samantha Marie Symphonie Pearl.
But she wasn't hungry.

Daddy changed Samantha Marie Symphonie Pearl.
But she didn't want to be changed.
She howled like the queen of the howler monkeys.

Even Granny couldn't find the off switch for the baby siren.
Then Sophie took off her space helmet and used her words.
"Give her to me, please!" said Sophie.

"Oh we can't do that," said Sophie's mama and daddy.
"Good idea," said Granny.
  Granny gave Samantha Marie Symphonie Pearl to Sophie.

Sophie used her words again as she sang to the baby.
No one could hear Sophie's words except her new baby sister.
Suddenly the room was quiet.

"What did you say?" asked Mama.
"What did you sing?" asked Daddy.
"Easy!" said Sophie.

"She wants to be called Jane.
So I sang to her, *Jane, Jane, don't be a pain!*
Now she's happy!"

"Now she's Jane!" said Granny.